If you have a home computer with Internet access you may:

- request an item to be placed on hold.
- renew an item that is not overdue or on hold.
- view titles and due dates checked out on your card.
- view and/or pay your outstanding fines online (over $5).

To view your patron record from your home computer click on Patchogue-Medford Library's homepage: **www.pmlib.org**

Published in 2010 by Windmill Books, LLC
303 Park Avenue South, Suite # 1280, New York, NY 10010-3657

Adaptations to North American Edition © 2010 Windmill Books

Published in 2006 by Autumn Publishing,
A division of Bonnier Media Ltd,
Chichester, West Sussex, PO20 7EQ, UK.
© 2006 Autumn Publishing

CREDITS:
Author: Sarah Nash
Illustrator: Andy Everitt-Stewart

Publisher Cataloging Data

Nash, Sarah
        Smelly blanket / written by Sarah Nash ; illustrated by Andy Everitt-Stewart.
                p. cm. – (Stories to grow with)
        Summary: Jake, his little brother, and his pets all have blankets with smells that remind them of good things.
        ISBN 978-1-60754-466-1(lib.) – ISBN 978-1-60754-467-8 (pbk.)
ISBN 978-1-60754-468-5 (6-pack)
        1. Blankets—Juvenile fiction   2. Odors—Juvenile fiction   [1. Blankets—Fiction   2. Smell—Fiction]   I. Everitt-Stewart, Andy
II. Title   III. Series
        [E]—dc22

Manufactured in the United States of America.

For more great fiction and nonfiction, go to windmillbooks.com.

Smelly Blanket

Written by Sarah Nash
Illustrated by Andy Everitt-Stewart

an imprint of
WINDMILL BOOKS™
New York

Jake loves his blanket.
He takes it with him wherever he goes.

Scruffy and Niffy love their blankets too.
Today Sam has come over to play.

"Phhhhwwwwoooooaaarrrr!" says Sam.
"Those blankets are SMELLY!"

"Shall I wash your blanket
and make it smell nice?"
asks Jake's mother.
"No thanks," says Jake.
"It doesn't like being washed."
He hugs the blanket tight.
"Washing makes it smell
like laundry detergent ... all
clean and YUCKY!"

While Jake and Sam are playing, Jake's mother sneaks Jake's blanket into the washing machine.
While Jake's mother is feeding Baby, Jake sneaks the blanket back.

Jake hides under a bush in the garden with Sam.
He sniffs his smelly blanket and tells Sam about all
the things it smells like:

Scruffy ...   ... and puddles ...

... and Grandma's
special biscuits!

While Scruffy is playing with Niffy, Jake's mother sneaks his blanket into the washing machine.

While Jake's mother is making lunch, Scruffy sneaks the blanket back.

Scruffy hides under the bush in the garden with Jake and Sam. He sniffs his smelly blanket.

It makes him think of bones ...

... and holes ...

... and chasing sticks!

While Niffy is washing her whiskers, Jake's mother sneaks her blanket into the washing machine.

While Jake's mother is washing the dishes, Niffy sneaks it back.

She hides under the bush in the garden with Jake and
Sam and Scruffy.
Niffy sniffs her smelly blanket.

It smells like cat treats ...   ... and mice ...

... and saucers of cream!

Jake's mother sneaks Baby's blanket while he is asleep.
She is putting it into the washing machine when...

Waaaaaaaaahhhhhhh!

Baby wants his blanket!

Jake's mother gives Baby his smelly blanket and he sniffs it.

It reminds him of cuddles ...

... and car rides ...

... and big brother Jake!

Jake's mother and Baby search for Jake and Sam
and Scruffy and Niffy.

They search upstairs.

They search downstairs.

Then they search in the garden.
"There you are!" says Jake's mother.

"Come on, you … out!" says Jake's mother. "If you won't let me wash your blankets, then let's give them a good airing!"

Jake's mother, Baby, Jake, Sam, Scruffy, and Niffy shake the blankets.

Up and down!

Round and round!

At last the blankets have all been aired.
Everyone flops down on the grass.

"I've had a lovely morning!" laughs Jake's mother.
"We may be smelly but at least we've had fun!" says Sam.

"I've had a lovely morning too," giggles Jake. "My blanket
is full of sunshine and laughter!"

"We've got the BEST smelliest blankets in the world!"